THE ABDUCTION OF AN EARL

THE LORDS OF THE ARISTOCRACY
BOOK 1

LINDA RAE SANDE

Twisted Teacup
PUBLISHING

ISBN: 978-1-946271-83-9

ALSO BY LINDA RAE SANDE

The Daughters of the Aristocracy

The Kiss of a Viscount

The Grace of a Duke

The Seduction of an Earl

The Sons of the Aristocracy

Tuesday Nights

The Widowed Countess

My Fair Groom

The Sisters of the Aristocracy

The Story of a Baron

The Passion of a Marquess

The Desire of a Lady

The Brothers of the Aristocracy

The Love of a Rake

The Caress of a Commander

The Epiphany of an Explorer

The Widows of the Aristocracy

The Gossip of an Earl

The Enigma of a Widow

The Secrets of a Viscount

The Widowers of the Aristocracy

The Dream of a Duchess

The Vision of a Viscountess

The Conundrum of a Clerk

The Charity of a Viscount

The Cousins of the Aristocracy

The Promise of a Gentleman

The Pride of a Gentleman

The Holidays of the Aristocracy

The Christmas of a Countess

The Knot of a Knight

The Holiday of a Marquess

The Snow Angel of a Duke

The Heirs of the Aristocracy

The Angel of an Astronomer

The Puzzle of a Bastard

The Choice of a Cavalier

The Bargain of a Baroness

The Jewel of an Earl's Heir

The Vixen of a Viscount

The Honor of an Heir

The Rose of a Sultan's Son

The Ladies of the Aristocracy

The Lady of a Grump

The Lady of a Sultan

The Wager of a Wallflower

The Lords of the Aristocracy

The Abduction of an Earl

Beyond the Aristocracy

The Pleasure of a Pirate

The Making of a Mistress

The Bride of a Baronet

The Caton of a Captain

Puss and Pots

The Betrothal of a Baron

The Abduction of an Earl

Stella of Akrotiri

Origins

Deminon

Diana

The Lyon's Den (Dragonblade Publishing)

The Courage of a Lyon

The Lady of a Lyon

Note: Translations of select titles are available in German, Italian, Spanish and Portuguese.

CHAPTER 1
A LADY SUFFERS A SURPRISE

April 1839, Weatherstone Manor, Mayfair

The last strains of the orchestra's final selection reached Persephone's ears when the dowager countess spotted her town coach and waved at the driver. He had managed to position her equipage in a most convenient location in the queue of other vehicles awaiting their owners in front of Weatherstone Manor, the Mayfair location known for always hosting the first ball of the Season.

Parker tipped his hat as he opened the coach door. "My lady," he said, offering his gloved hand in assistance.

"You know me too well if you've timed your arrival for this very moment," Persephone commented as she placed a silk-gloved hand in his and took the step up and into the velvet-lined coach.

"I never left, my lady," he replied. "Nice night to watch the stars." He closed the door before his mistress could reply and then bounded up and onto the driver's seat. A moment later, and the coach pulled away from the pavement.

Persephone settled into the blue velvet squabs and sighed in relief as she extracted her feet from her dance slippers. Wiggling her toes, she had a thought to simply leave her shoes off when it was time to make her way into March House. Who would notice if she entered the townhouse barefoot?

In the middle of taking a deep breath, she stopped and sniffed. The air inside the coach bore an unfamiliar scent. A cologne unlike anything her late husband had worn. Walter's usual *parfum* brought to mind leather and musk, a rather manly odor for a gentleman who wasn't.

This cologne was spicy. Citrusy. She sniffed again and then gave a start when the sound of a snore suddenly filled the coach.

"Who's there?" she asked in alarm as she straightened on the bench.

A snuffle-snort was followed by a moan and a groan and a "bloody hell."

Stuffing her feet back into her dance slippers, she pressed herself as far into the corner of the coach as she could. "I say again, who is there?" she asked, managing to sound more annoyed than frightened.

"Where the hell am I?" a male voice asked from the other side of the coach. From the way the prone form moved—a long lump rising on one side—Persephone realized the man had been sleeping and was now propped up on an elbow. She reached over to the window curtain and drew it back so the light from the coach lantern illuminated the interior.

"Ack!" the man complained as he lifted a hand to shield his face from the sudden glare.

Persephone gasped. "Lord... Lord Wilmington? Is that you?" She dropped the curtain, but the gathered panel remained parted enough to allow some light into the coach.

Another moan and groan sounded as he moved to sit up, although his head ended up in his hands as his elbows rested on his knees. "If I am, you have my permission to shoot me. Put me out of my misery," he whispered hoarsely. The coach jerked hard when the wheel dipped into a hole left from a missing cobble, and he barked a curse.

"Lord Wilmington?" she repeated.

He lifted his head and regarded her in the dim light. "You have me at a disadvantage, my lady," he said.

"Jack, it's me. Persephone March," she replied. "What are you doing in my coach?" Other than the sound of the spinning wheels and the clopping of hooves on the cobbles, there was silence for a time, and she wondered if the intruder had passed out.

"Your coach?" he murmured before he groaned again.

"Whatever is wrong with you?"

Jack straightened and allowed his head to fall back

onto the top of the squabs. "What day is this? It feels as if I've drunk an entire bottle of brandy. And not a good one, either." One of his hands went to the side of his head to hold it, as if it required assistance in remaining on his neck.

"It's the first Tuesday after Easter," she replied. "Lord Weatherstone's ball?" she added, sure that would give him enough information to sort his loss of time.

"I... I don't recall being there," he murmured before he inhaled sharply. "Wait. Yes, I do. I arrived at the same time as the Marquess of Reading," he commented. "I remember being thirsty... went for the punch..." He straightened. "That's it. Someone must have poured a good deal of brandy into the punch," he stated.

Persephone scoffed as she leaned forward in an attempt to get a closer look at her passenger. "Jack, trust me when I tell you the punch was definitely not spiked. A bit too much orgeat, but... there were no spirits in it," she said as she placed a hand beneath his chin and lifted it slightly. "Although you do *look* as if you're drunk," she accused.

"I feel like I was," he replied, grasping her hand to bring it to his lips. He pressed a kiss on the back of it. "Not now, though." He let go of her hand, and Persephone quickly pulled it away.

Jack pushed his hand over his head, his fingers leaving furrows in his dark hair as a wince crossed his handsome features. "If it wasn't alcohol, then how do you explain this splitting headache? And my tongue feels as if it..."

He paused, his grimace accompanying a most unpleasant sound.

"If you're going to be sick—"

"I am not," he assured her. "But I do think I've been... poisoned or... or drugged or something," he murmured, his eyes narrowing as he seemed to struggle to remember anything from earlier that evening.

Persephone inhaled sharply. "By whom?" she asked in alarm.

"Well, if I knew that..." he murmured, his gaze going to the coach window nearest him. "Good God, what time is it?"

Her blonde brows furrowing in concern, Persephone said, "About two, I think."

"In the morning?" Jack countered, straightening on the bench seat. He hissed as his other hand joined the first in holding his head.

"Yes. Shall I have Parker take you to your apartments? Are you still at The Albany?" She started to reach up to tap on the trap door, but Jack intercepted her hand.

"No need, my lady," he replied, placing his other hand over the top of hers so he could hold onto it. "Might I be allowed to join you this evening? At least until I can sort what happened?"

Persephone inhaled softly, surprised at how he held her hand. He had done so in the past the very same way. A long time ago, when he had proposed marriage. Since she had already been forced by her father to accept the

Earl of Castlewait's offer of a marriage of convenience, she'd had to decline Jack's offer.

At least she'd had the benefit of a few months of Jack's attentions. A few months of young love and stolen moments. Despite the intervening twenty years, Jack still sported his handsome good looks, although these days he appeared a bit rough around the edges. His face, tanned from daily horseback rides, displayed creases on the sides of his eyes, and a scar from a wound he'd suffered due to the tip of a fencing foil marred his right cheek. The hair near his temples was nearly white, and his usual black hair was peppered with strands of gray.

The thought of him spending the night with her at March House had flutterbies dancing about in Persephone's stomach. They hadn't been together in a bed since the week after he'd taken her virtue all those years ago. "Of course you can stay," she finally replied. "As long as you need."

He nodded and then winced as the slight movement seemed to cause him pain. "I'll be a perfect gentleman," he said. "I promise."

Persephone frowned. "And what if I don't want you to be?" she asked in a whisper, barely loud enough to be heard over the sound of the coach wheels on the cobbles.

His eyes narrowed, and Jack allowed a wan grin. "Is that... is that an invitation?"

Her confidence faltered. "Would you accept it?" she countered. "Or have I grown too old for your tastes these days?"

For a moment, she wished she could have taken back her last words. But Jack Kirkpatrick, Earl of Wilmington, had a reputation of late. One that proclaimed he preferred younger widows and virgins. His name was synonymous with words like *scoundrel* and *rake* and *libertine*. His initials were frequently to be found in the articles printed in *The Tattler*, London's premier gossip news-sheet.

"Don't believe everything you hear, Sephie," he replied, tightening his hold on her hand. "Or read. And you'll never be too old for me."

Persephone grinned at hearing his pet name for her. No one but him had called her 'Sephie', not in her entire life.

"Damn, but I wish I felt better, because I'd really like to prove myself to you right now."

Excitement at hearing his claim had Persephone's insides reacting much like they had two decades ago. Merely seeing the earl filled her with desire. It was no wonder he'd been able to coax her onto a bed and have his way with her. That fact that he had known exactly what to do to incite frissons of pleasure back then had her happy to offer hospitality now. "Perhaps in the morning," she whispered.

"I'd like that," he replied.

The coach came to a stuttering halt, and the countess scoffed. "Well, I do believe we're about to shock Parker. That is, if he didn't know you climbed into my coach."

Jack furrowed a brow, an expression of worry

crossing his face. "I... I don't remember getting into this coach," he said, his voice once again betraying his confusion. Then his eyes rounded. "Did you... did *you* arrange this? Did you have me drugged?"

Persephone scoffed, momentarily offended he would think such a thing. "I rather I wish I did, but no, I assure you, it was not me," she said on a sigh. "I would have hoped you would come of your own accord, if I'd sent you an invitation."

His eyes narrowing briefly, Jack considered her words. "I would have," he whispered.

The coach door opened and Persephone, heartened by his response to her last comment, allowed her driver to help her down the step. He was about to close the door, but she held up a staying hand. "Tell me, Parker. You said you didn't drive away from Weatherstone Manor the entire night?"

The driver gave a start. "That's because I didn't, my lady. Just... I just stargazed all night," he said on a shrug.

"Were you *always* with the coach?"

Parker's eyes darted to the side. "I... I might have stepped away a few times. To get a better view of the sky," he admitted in a halting voice. "There's a rather large tree on the one side of the Weatherstone property. It was in the way."

"So... no one gave you any coins to look the other direction or... or to take on a passenger?" Persephone pressed.

His eyes rounding in confusion, Parker shook his

head. "No, my lady. Nor would I have accepted," he claimed.

"All right then—"

"There were a couple whom I thought seemed out of place, though," he added as his gaze turned to his mind's eye. "A... a few hours ago."

Persephone's gaze darted to the interior of the coach. "What do you mean?" she asked, well aware Jack had moved closer to the door so he could listen in on her conversation with the driver.

"They wasn't dressed right for a ball, is all. I just thought they was there to watch the arrivals like some of the common folk do. But usually the onlookers take their leave after most of the guests have arrived, and they were still there after you went into the house."

"Oh?" she responded. "This couple... when did they leave?"

Parker shrugged. "I didn't take note, my lady, but it might have been about the time a gentleman was leading another out of the house. Drunk, like. Dressed all fine, but stumbling about, barely able to walk."

Persephone's eyes rounded. "Would you recognize the gentleman if you saw him again?" she asked, just as Jack emerged from the coach.

Parker gasped, one hand going to his chest before he stepped between his mistress and Jack, as if he intended to provide protection. "It's *you*. The drunkard," he said in shock.

"*Drugged* would be the more appropriate word,"

Jack remarked, directing a look of annoyance at him. "Any idea who escorted me out of Weatherstone Manor?" he asked. "Was it just one person? Or two?"

Shaking his head, Parker glanced back at Persephone. "Just the one. I haven't seen him 'afore," he said. "But he was about your age, I think. Seemed to know you, given how he was talkin' to you. Cursin' at you, mostly."

Jack winced but didn't say anything.

"Was this man you speak of... was he dressed for the ball?" Persephone asked.

Parker furrowed his brows and thought for a moment. "Well, yes. Dressed as fine as you, sir," he said with a nod to Jack. "He didn't have a hat on, though. But you did."

Persephone and Jack exchanged quick glances. "I don't remember that," Jack said. He poked his head back into the coach, and after a moment of rummaging around, he emerged with a top hat in one hand. "Well, it's a hat, but it's not mine," he murmured.

"How can you be sure?" Persephone asked. The black beaver looked like any fashionable men's top hat of late.

Jack turned it over and aimed it so the coach lantern could illuminate the label inside the hat band. "I only buy hats from *Fitzsimmons and Smith* in Oxford Street," he said. The label in the hat he held was for a shop in New Bond Street. "Which means my hat is probably still back at Weatherstone Manor."

"Or the man who escorted you out of the house has

it," Parker said, obviously intrigued by the unusual events of the evening.

"Perhaps a good night's sleep will have your memory returning, Lord Wilmington," Persephone suggested. She turned to Parker. "If you remember anything else about what you saw this evening, will you please let me know? Or... or tell Bentley?" she said, referring to the butler of March House. She took Jack's proffered arm.

"Of course, my lady," Parker replied. "Will you be needing the coach again tonight?"

Chuckling, Persephone shook her head. "Of course not."

The driver hesitated, obviously bothered that he was unaware of the earl's presence in the coach. "If you'd like, I can go back to Weatherstone Manor," he offered. "Ask about his lordship's hat. And return this one at the same time," he added, pointing to the hat Jack still held.

Persephone inhaled softly and turned to gauge Jack's response. When he merely shrugged, she said, "That's very kind of you." She was about to fish a few coins from a pocket in her gown, but Jack beat her to it, pulling several from his waistcoat pocket. He gave them to the driver.

"Be sure to give a coin or two to the footman who assists you," he said. "Especially if he shares any news with you."

"I will, my lord," Parker said as he took the hat.

"Should you acquire Lord Wilmington's hat, simply leave it on the hall table if Bentley is no longer up and about," Persephone requested, deciding she didn't wish to be disturbed. Although she sensed Jack's growing unease, she knew he needed to sleep off the effects of the drug—or whatever is was that had him so discombobulated.

"Yes, my lady."

"Good night, Parker."

"Good night, my lady," the driver replied, watching as Lord Wilmington lead Lady Castlewait to the front door. He hurried back to the coach and set the horses in motion.

CHAPTER 2
AN ABDUCTION GONE AWRY

*M*eanwhile, in Cheapside

"What the hell do you mean you *lost* him?" Baron Abraham Kravets asked, pacing before the desk in his study. "He drank the punch, didn't he?"

"Yes, sir, he did."

"And?"

Elias Turnbridge winced. "I got him out of there, mostly unseen."

"What do you mean, *mostly*?" Kravets asked, his annoyance evident. He had stopped in his tracks, the worn carpet beneath his feet no longer able to swallow the sound of a creaking floorboard.

"I think there might have been too much of that sleeping powder in the glass of punch, and he drank it all in a single gulp," Elias explained. "It took effect right quick, and, well, I had to get him up the stairs and out of there by way of the front door."

The baron gave a start. "You were supposed to go through the gardens," Kravets said, resuming his pacing. The floorboard once again creaked in protest. "What were you *thinking*?"

Displaying a wince, Elias seemed unsure of how to respond. "The ballroom was a crush, sir," he replied. "Always is, from what I heard some people say. There was no way to get him past so many guests without drawing notice of his condition."

"So... what happened then?"

Elias rolled his eyes. "A footman helped me get him out the door. Gave me a hat..." He paused, a grimace forming when he wondered if the hat had indeed been the earl's. "So I put that on him," he explained. Another wince crossed his face when he realized his final departure from the manor house by way of the gardens, about an hour later, meant his own hat was still at Weatherstone Manor. He would have to make a trip back to Park Lane to retrieve it. "Once we were out of doors, I turned him over to the two you hired to watch for us. They held him in the dark next to some bushes until I got back to the front door. Before I stepped back into the house, I saw 'em put Wilmington into the coach. By then, he was completely out, sir."

Kravets stomped a booted foot on the Turkish carpet, which had Elias jerking in response. From the awful sound the floorboard made, it might have cracked in protest. "Well, he wasn't *in* the coach that arrived here at eleven o'clock now, was he?"

Sighing, Elias rubbed a hand over one side of his face. He didn't know if Wilmington was or wasn't in the coach. He had still been in the ballroom at Weatherstone Manor at that time. "I don't see how he could have regained consciousness and escaped the coach, sir, which means..." His eyes widened and he swallowed. "They must have put him in the *wrong coach*," he whispered.

Kravets jerked back as if he'd been punched in the jaw. "What the hell did you say?"

Elias swallowed again. "Well, there was a whole line of carriages pulled up along Park Lane this evening," he said. "Most of them bearing their owners' coat of arms. They must have misread the Kravets family crest and put him into the wrong coach," he reasoned.

Kravets brows had furrowed into one long graying brow, and beneath it, his eyes blazed with fury. "*Idiots*," he hissed. "Did you see the driver?"

"Sir?"

"The driver of the coach you saw them putting him into... did you see the driver?"

Furrowing his brows, Elias struggled to remember everything he could about the coach. About the horses. Although it was a fairly dark night—he didn't recall seeing the moon—there had been a string of Japanese lanterns lining the pavement up to the manor. The light they gave off didn't do much to illuminate the space beyond the pavers, though. The scent of rain had hung in the air due to the low layer of gray clouds that were slowly clearing to reveal a sky full of stars, so everything not lit by the lanterns had appeared in shades of black and gray.

"There was no driver on the bench, sir," Elias murmured. "The four horses were all black... or a very dark gray," he added. "The crest was in gold, but it was too far away for me to make out the details."

"Shite," Kravets cursed. "My driver was specifically told not to leave his post and to be ready to depart no later than half-past-ten."

"I had Wilmington out there at quarter past the hour. I know because I checked my chronometer when I returned to the ballroom, and it wasn't even half-past," Elias explained. He grimaced before asking, "Was *anyone* in the coach, sir?"

Kravets' face once again reddened with rage. "Of course not."

Elias scoffed. "Your driver didn't check to see that he had a passenger before he left?" From the tone of his voice, it was obvious he thought the driver was at fault.

"He was told not leave his post. Not even to take a piss," Kravets countered. He inhaled as his gaze went to the coffered ceiling above. "Coach-and-four, black horses, no driver," he murmured. "With a crest similar to mine."

Unfamiliar with most of the crests of the aristocratic families, Elias knew he would be of no help in identifying the coach holding Jack Kirkpatrick, Earl of Wilmington. "I rather doubt the earl will regain consciousness before the morning," he said.

"Which means someone will discover him in their coach. A few will have left the ball by now. Surely they raised an alarm," Kravets said, his eyes suddenly widening. "The Weatherstone footmen will be the first to know." He pulled out his chronometer and checked the time. "Oh. It's barely two o'clock. If you leave now, you can be there before most of the guests have even departed," he said with some excitement. "The orchestra is probably still playing, and the card room will no doubt be occupied until the sun comes up."

"Yes, sir," Elias replied. "Should I go in your coach?"

Kravets sighed. "It's parked out front. Renner knew enough not to put it away for the night," he said, referring to his driver. The poor man had looked as if he might die of fright when his master had cursed and kicked the coach wheel upon discovering there was no passenger inside.

"Very good, sir," Elias replied. He gave a slight bow and hurried out of Kravets' office, obviously relieved to be out of the baron's sight.

CHAPTER 3
AN EXCHANGE OF HATS

*M*eanwhile, in Park Lane

Determined to do his part to discover what might have happened to Lord Wilmington, Lady Castlewait's driver, Parker, had the Castlewait coach-and-four speeding down Park Lane faster than he had ever driven in his life. He thrilled at the sensation of air blowing over his face, and he knew the horses were enjoying the opportunity to run for a few minutes.

Expecting to find the street nearly deserted in front of Weatherstone Manor, Parker was surprised to discover nearly a dozen coaches still lined up. The first ball of the Season had not only attracted a large number of guests for the ball, but those who enjoyed playing cards until dawn.

Parking the equipage at the end of the line of coaches, he retrieved the top hat from inside the coach—

he had placed it on a bench in the event of rain—and made his way to the front door.

As a servant, he was used to having to enter houses using the servants' door in the back. Given his assignment, he felt it necessary to use the front door, and he was relieved when a couple exited only a moment before he would have used the brass knocker. He stepped in, giving a nod to an ancient butler who was helping another gentleman into a coat.

Noticing several footmen guarding shelves of hats and hooks containing all manner of outerwear, he approached the first one who nodded to him.

"Good evening. It seems his lordship was given the wrong hat when he took his leave earlier." He offered the beaver to the footman. "He wondered if his might still be here. A bit taller, black, and made by *Fitzsimmons and Smith*," he added.

The footman's eyes rounded at the mention of the hat maker in Oxford Street. "Ah, the hat that makes the gentleman," the servant said, quoting the hat maker's motto. He took the errant hat and placed it on a table while he checked under the hats of those that were lined up on a shelf. "Your master is in luck, if this is it," he said as he brought the hat to Parker. "It's the only one with an 'F and S' label," he added.

With no other means of identifying the hat, Parker gave the footman a nod. "I'm sure this must be it. You'll see to it the rightful owner gets the other one?"

"Of course... if he hasn't already left. Though he's

probably in the card parlor. Since the orchestra stopped playing a few minutes ago, most of the guests have taken their leave."

Parker nodded his understanding but paused. He was tempted to mention the issue of Lord Wilmington, but instead said, "Tell me... did you happen to see a man escorting another out the door? He might have appeared... drunk?"

The taller man scoffed. "Had a few of those this evening," he said with a grin. "But it was odd when the first one happened so early."

"Oh?" Parker responded. Interested to learn more, he leaned in closer. "Do you happen to remember when that might have... happened?"

The footmen screwed up his face in concentration. "Oh, mayhap ten o'clock? The receiving line had broken up by then, of course," he replied. "Can't say I recognized either of the gents, though." His eyes rounded. "But I do remember only one of them had a hat when they went out the door." He winced. "I would have gone after them, but I'm not allowed to leave my post."

"I understand," Parker replied, disappointed the servant couldn't provide more information.

"It has been a night of excitement, I must say," the footman remarked.

Parker furrowed a brow. "Oh? Something besides drunkards having to be escorted out?"

"Oh, aye. Lord JW was caught kissing a young lady behind a hedgerow," the footman whispered. "Ever since he returned from his Grand Tour, the rake's been having 'is way with the chits at every entertainment."

His eyes rounding at hearing this bit of news, Parker was about to ask if the footman knew the identity of Lord JW, but a marquess stepped up to request his hat and coat. Parker handed over the coins Lord Wilmington had given him. "For your trouble," he said.

"Thank you," the footman replied, an appreciative expression appeared on his long face. "G'night."

Noting the butler was no longer near the front door, Parker tucked the top hat under one arm and let himself out. He was deep in thought when he nearly collided with another gentleman. "Pardon, sir," he said as he stepped aside.

He was about to continue on the Japanese lantern-lined path when he realized the man wore no hat. Despite a second glance, he didn't recognize the gentleman and so hurried on his way to the Castlewait coach. Disappointment settled over him at not learning the identity of whoever had removed Lord Wilmington from the ball.

At least he had secured the earl's hat.

CHAPTER 4
A MYSTERY DEEPENS

*M*eanwhile, *back at March House*

The butler, Bentley, had the hunter green front door opened before Persephone and Jack stepped up to it.

"There's been an incident this evening, Bentley," Persephone stated as she sailed into the hall and turned to allow the servant to help her with her mantle. "Someone attempted to abduct Lord Wilmington from the ball this evening, but they put him into the wrong coach," she said, her words the first to describe what she had come to realize was the only explanation for what had happened that evening. "Is the master suite ready for a guest? His lordship is in need of quarters for the night."

Bentley's usual bored expression was replaced with one of alarm. "It is, of course, my lady. Should I send Carlisle to fetch a constable? Or... or a Bow Street Runner?" he asked, referring to one of the footmen.

Jack exchanged a quick glance with Persephone and shook his head. "That won't be necessary, although I may see to it myself in the morning," he murmured.

"Will you require a valet, sir?"

Once again, Jack shook his head and then winced at having made his headache worse. "I can dress myself, but I really could use a glass of water," he said.

"I'll bring up a pitcher and a glass to the bedchamber right away," Bentley replied.

"I can escort you to your room," Persephone offered before she turned her attention back to Bentley. "No one outside of this household can know Lord Wilmington is here," she stated firmly. "Do I make myself clear, Bentley? No one can know. His life may in danger," she stated, now sure she was speaking the truth. "And tell Cooper I won't be needing her this evening," she added, referring to her lady's maid.

His brows rising nearly to his hairline, Bentley swallowed. "Of course, my lady. I shan't tell anyone he's here."

Persephone hooked her arm into Jack's and led him to the staircase set off to one side of the hall. She was aware of his attention on her and sensed he wished to speak, but she didn't say anything until they were at the top of the stairs. "What is it?" she asked in a whisper.

"I don't recall seeing *you* at the ball tonight," he said as they moved to climb the next flight of stairs to the second floor. "I'm sure I would remember, given your gown," he added. "You always look stunning in blue."

Glancing down at her sapphire blue ballgown, Persephone huffed. "It would have been far more memorable if it had been the only one of its style and color," she groused. "I saw similar gowns on at least three other ladies tonight," she complained. "I was rather late with my arrival, though. Ten o'clock or shortly thereafter."

"Oh?" he replied. "What kept you?"

"I despise having to go through a receiving line, and Lord and Lady Weatherstone must be the last aristocrats in Mayfair who insist on greeting their guests before they're announced at the top of the stairs," she complained. "I had hoped to avoid it—"

"Why?" he asked. They were stopped in front of a door near the end of a corridor.

"I had no one to escort me this evening," she stated before she turned the door handle and pushed the dark wood panel open to reveal the master bedchamber. She moved to an ebony dresser and opened the top drawer. "Once I'm in the ballroom, I'm fine. It's always such a crush... but they were still greeting guests when I arrived. I had the unenviable honor of being the last one in line." She pulled a nightshirt from the drawer and shook it out before her eyes rounded.

"What is it?" Jack asked, noticing her alarm. He glanced around the room, expecting to find something wrong. The bedchamber seemed in perfect order, though, and the stale odor of disuse wasn't evident in the air.

"Do you remember if the receiving line was still in

place when you were taken from the house?" she asked, her attention still on her mind's eye as she absently handed him the nightshirt.

Not expecting the query, Jack scoffed. "I don't think my... my *abductor* would have used that route if they..." He clamped his mouth shut.

"What?" she asked, reaching up to undo the knot in his cravat.

"The receiving line couldn't have been there because I remember seeing Weatherstone *in* the ballroom. When I went to get a drink," he murmured. "That means the receiving line had broken up before... *before* I was drugged."

Persephone considered his comment for a moment as she unwrapped the silk from around his neck. "Do you remember going up the stairs?" she asked, moving to undo his topcoat buttons.

Bentley appeared at the door, which was still open. He carried a silver salver on which rested a pitcher of water and a crystal glass. "Your water, sir," he said, setting the tray on the dresser. He poured a glass and offered it to the earl. "I've taken the liberty of requesting hot washing water be brought up for you. It's to be delivered to her ladyship's bathing chamber," he explained in a quiet voice, nodding his head in the direction of a door in the corner of the room. "So no one will know you are here."

"Thank you, Bentley," Jack replied before he downed the entire glass in a few gulps. He closed his eyes a few moments before taking a deep breath. "That's better," he whispered.

"Will there be anything else, my lady?" the butler asked, his attention on his mistress. He refilled the glass of water.

"I think that should do it," she replied. "I appreciate your discretion, and I rather doubt we'll be in need of your services before noon," she added quietly. "I'm sure his lordship will wish to sleep off the effects of the drug."

"Very good, my lady." Bentley took his leave, although he didn't shut the door.

Sensing Jack was going to ask about the room arrangements, Persephone said, "The mistress and master suites are connected by way of the bathing chamber..." she waved to the corner door, "...and the dressing room," she added, pointing to a door adjacent to the main door. "If you have everything you need, I'll go to my room now," she said, moving to the still-open door.

Jack reached out and gently hooked a hand around her elbow. When she turned, her eyes met his as she furrowed a brow. "I'll have everything you need if you join me in here," he said in a whisper. "I may not last long..." He let the sentence trail off before he sighed in frustration.

Persephone inhaled softly. "All right," she replied, her pulse accelerating at the thought of spending the night in bed with Jack. Even if they only held one another, it would be a welcome change from sleeping alone. "Lock your door. I'll be about a half-hour," she said. "You'll no doubt hear the footman when he arrives with the water."

"Thank you, Sephie," he replied, pulling her into his arms. He kissed her softly. Slowly. And when he finally pulled away, he left his forehead pressed to hers. "You would never believe how much I have wanted to do that."

A slow smile lifting the corners of her lips, Persephone whispered, "Perhaps you can endeavor to convince me in a half-hour?" Without waiting for a reply, she turned and left the bedchamber, pulling the door shut behind her.

CHAPTER 5
A FOOTMAN AND A HAT

ack at Baron Kravets' townhouse Elias cursed under his breath as he rushed up to the Kravets' town coach. "Back to Weatherstone Manor," he called up to Renner. "And hurry."

The startled driver, who looked to be no older than seventeen, nodded. "Yes, sir."

Before Elias had a chance to shut the coach door and be seated, the equipage jerked into motion. He cursed again as he settled into the shabby leather squabs, his nose wrinkling when he smelled the odors of cheroot smoke and unwashed bodies. For at least the tenth time that evening, he regretted having agreed to be part of Abraham Kravets plan to avenge his daughter's honor.

Like most who read the gossip found in the pages of *The Tattler*, Kravets assumed the rake referred to as *Lord JW* was John "Jack" Kirkpatrick, Earl of Wilmington.

After reading the latest issue, which included an

article describing a scandalous incident that took place during a *musicale* at Worthington House, Kravets was convinced his daughter, Honoria, had been ruined by one *Lord JW*. He had been sure there could be no other young lady matching the article's description but her.

As a means to see to it the earl was held responsible for his rakish behavior, Kravets set about planning his revenge—drug and abduct the man from an early Season entertainment, haul him to Kravets' townhouse, wake him up with a right cross to his jaw, and inform him he was to marry Honoria by special license the following day.

Kravets still hadn't decided if her dowry would be paid or not.

Honoria had yet to speak to her father. When he confronted her on the matter, she immediately turned into a watering pot and claimed she didn't know the man who ravished her in an alcove at Worthington House. She didn't even deny the event had occurred.

Her mother and Kravets' baroness, Lady Margaret Kravets, was doing her best to claim that the young lady described in the news-sheet could not possibly be her daughter since Honoria had been with her at the time of the so-called ruination and that they had not even been in attendance at the *musicale*. "We weren't there because we weren't invited," she told her husband.

As for those who had claimed to have seen the baroness at the *musicale*, she would tell them that

Honoria wasn't with her that evening but had stayed home complaining of a megrim.

Kravets wasn't convinced.

Sure Honoria was protecting the identity of her lover, he had called upon his new friend and business partner Elias Turnbridge to help with his plan.

Not expecting the baron to concoct such an elaborate scheme involving a drugging and an abduction, Elias had agreed to go along with whatever Kravets planned. He only meant to appease the man because they were business partners. He feared the baron might pull out of funding his latest venture and force him to have to line up another investor.

Now Elias wished he had left town with the excuse that he had business in the country. Or, better yet, another country.

When the Kravets coach stuttered to a halt down the street from Weatherstone Manor, Elias was relieved to see a number of coaches still lined up along Park Lane. Stepping out of the equipage, he paused to examine the baron's coat of arms on the door.

At first glance, he thought it looked like any other coat of arms. It was painted in gold. There was a shield. There were supporters. There was a crest. And across the bottom was a motto in Latin on an open-scroll banner.

He studied the details more closely before making his way to the next parked coach. He nearly stopped when he saw that the crest on its door had the motto at the top. The supporters were a pair of dragons.

When he passed the next coach, he lingered for a moment, pretending to adjust his cravat in the reflection from the coach window. That coat of arms had dogs as supporters and the motto was emblazoned at the bottom.

Coming upon the lanterns leading to the front door of Weatherstone Manor, Elias nearly bumped into a man who had just left the residence.

"Pardon, sir," the younger man said, the style of his caped coat and top hat that of a driver. He seemed to stutter-step and do a double-take before continuing on his way to a coach parked farther down Park Lane.

Curious at the driver's odd behavior, Elias lifted a hand to remove his hat and was reminded that he wore no hat.

No wonder the driver had given him such an odd look!

Elias hurried into the house and immediately came to a halt when he recognized his hat among the half-dozen a footman was rearranging on a shelf. When another footman turned from giving a coat to a departing guest, he said, "Yes, sir?"

"I'm here to collect my hat," Elias said.

"Of course, sir. Must have been some game going on in the card parlor this evening."

Relieved the footman hadn't seen him come in by way of the front door, Elias merely shrugged. "No more than usual, I suppose," he replied. "Tell me... have there been any reports of aa gentleman being found in the wrong coach this evening?"

The footman blinked. "Sir?"

"Any... guests... making a fuss out front?" Elias hedged.

Pulling his head back so his chin doubled, the rather tall servant seemed to think on it a moment before he glanced about and then leaned in closer. "A young lady was caught being kissed by that Lord JW behind a hedgerow in the gardens out back," he hoarsely whispered. "But I haven't heard about anything amiss out front," he added in a quiet voice.

Elias gave a start. "Lord JW?" he repeated in a whisper. "When... when was this?"

"Oh, it's been hours ago, sir. Probably around midnight, if not 'afore." His eyes suddenly widened. "It was definitely 'afore midnight. Supper hadn't yet been served." The servant grinned, apparently pleased with his powers of deduction.

Elias furrowed his brows. Given the amount of sleeping powder he had dumped into Lord Wilmington's punch, he was sure the man could not have awakened, made his way out of a coach and into the house, descended the stairs to the ballroom, flirted with a young lady, and escorted her to the Weatherstone gardens for a tryst—despite his reputation as a rake.

Besides, Elias had been standing near the open French doors to the garden for nearly an hour *after* he put Wilmington into the coach. With the number of guests in the ballroom—the Weatherstone ball was always a crush—he needed the fresh air. Surely he would have seen Wilmington if the earl had exited by way of the French doors.

"You mentioned you were here to claim your hat, sir?" the footman prompted.

Pulled from his reverie, Elias nodded. "That one right there on the end," he said as nodded to his beaver.

The footman blinked again. "Oy. If you had come any sooner, it wouldn't have been here for you, sir."

Elias frowned. "Whatever do you mean?"

Aware he might be speaking ill of one of his fellow footmen, the servant lowered his voice and said, "It was mistakenly given to another gentleman, sir, but it's been returned and exchanged for the correct one." He lifted the hat between two sets of fingers and held it out to Elias. "It doesn't appear to have suffered, sir. You'll want to check the label just to be sure it is yours."

Turning the hat over, Elias confirmed it was the beaver he had purchased in New Bond Street only the week before. "When... when was it returned?" he asked. "And by whom?"

The footman had already begun searching for another guest's coat but said, "Oh, only a moment ago, sir. By a driver. Don't know his name, though."

Elias inhaled sharply. "Do you know whose driver?"

Appearing to think on it for a moment, the footman shook his head. "Can't say as I've ever seen 'im 'afore."

Tossing the footman a coin, Elias rushed out of the

house in search of the driver he had passed on his way into the house.

34

CHAPTER 6
A FORMER SPY CONFESSES MUCH

*M*eanwhile, at the Castlewait townhouse

Jack regarded the nightshirt Persephone had given him with a wince. He rarely wore one to bed now that he was back in London. These days, he didn't have to spend his nights half-dressed and be ready to move on a moment's notice.

When he was assigned to a small unit of agents in the Kingdom of the Netherlands, he had grown used to settling on an uncomfortable cot or on the ground, rarely able to enjoy a full night of sleep. As an aristocrat and an officer in the military, he would have been provided a private tent and a clerk or two to see to it he wasn't disturbed.

As a spy, he didn't have that luxury.

For the past two decades, he had thrilled at carrying out the clandestine assignments. Excitement at receiving new orders had him looking forward to donning disguises and traveling incognito. Intercepting enemy orders and decoding their messages had provided a daily dose of adrenaline and provided him a sense of purpose his position as Earl of Wilmington couldn't begin to match.

Now... now he was glad to have his days of deception behind him. Only a month ago, his last assignment in Belgium had resulted in what the Foreign Office was sure would be a turning point in the war against Napoleon and the French.

Although he had suffered a slight wound from a bayonet, he was otherwise undamaged. Despite assurances he could continue his work on the Continent, he received orders claiming his cover was blown and that his services would no longer be required by the Crown.

He had returned to British shores dressed as a commoner. Arrived at his apartment in The Albany finding it much the way he had left it. Resumed life as an aristocrat.

Discovered he hadn't been missed.

He hadn't been missed because either someone had taken to pretending to be him, or he was a victim of mistaken identity.

His reputation as a rake, one he hadn't suffered since before he had inherited the earldom nearly twenty years ago, had returned thanks to someone who had his initials.

Lord JW.

Through no fault of his own, he was suddenly back

in the gossip pages. Rumors claimed he was deflowering virgins and having his way with young widows despite his absence from Society. Given he hadn't been with a woman since his return to England, he couldn't decide whether he was amused or annoyed by the situation.

Well, after what had happened tonight, he certainly wasn't amused.

Tossing his coats and shirt onto the back of a chair before removing his shoes and stockings, he headed into the bathing chamber. A candle lamp provided more than enough light to see by given the size of the mirror over a dressing table. Another mirror hung over a console on which a ceramic bowl and a pitcher sat. Steam poured forth from the pitcher as he emptied its contents into the bowl. He helped himself to a linen cloth and doused it in the water. Sighing with satisfaction as he washed his face and chest, Jack was about to help himself to a bath linen when he realized he wasn't alone.

He stepped to the side to discover Persephone's reflection next to his in the mirror.

"I apologize. I didn't mean to interrupt," she said in a quiet voice.

Jack couldn't help his body's reaction to seeing her again, especially given her mode of dress. She wore only a thin silk wrapper tied at the waist, the fabric doing nothing to hide the swell of her breasts or hips nor the dark triangle at the apex of her thighs.

"You're not interrupting," he murmured. He rubbed the linen over his face and chest, well aware her gaze had settled on the once-black hair that covered most of his chest. The graying, crisp curls tapered to a thin line of dark hair that disappeared behind the top of his black breeches. "You're a very welcome sight, in fact."

Persephone approached him, one hand landing on his chest as she lifted her face to his. Their kiss was quick but thorough, and when she pulled away to allow her gaze to sweep over the rest of his body, she winced. "What happened here?" she asked in alarm, her finger darting to where the bayonet had glanced off a rib.

"A frog got me," he replied. "Before I could kill him."

From her immediate reaction, Jack knew she had jumped to the wrong conclusion. "I did a stint on the Continent. I've only been back in England a few weeks."

Persephone furrowed a brow. "How... how is that possible?" she asked in a whisper.

He kissed her forehead and led her into the master suite. The bed linens had been turned down, the expanse of white an overt invitation. "Tell me, when is the last time you remember actually *seeing* me here in London?" he asked, his own memory that of a night he attended the theatre with his mother while Persephone had been escorted by her husband.

Her brows furrowing, Persephone looked as if she was about to respond and then scoffed. "I suppose it was that night at the theatre. About a week before... before Castlewait died," she stammered. "You were escorting Countess Wilmington, as I recall."

"I had already received orders to go to the Continent," he said as he turned down the flame on the room's only candle lamp. "I left England two days later."

Persephone inhaled softly. "I didn't know you were in the army," she said as she sat on the edge of the bed.

"I wasn't," he stated. He had moved to the darkest corner of the room while he undid the fastenings at the top of his breeches. Pushing them down along with his smalls, he stepped out of the garments, well aware Persephone watched in fascination.

She'd had the very same expression on her face the first time she had watched him undress. One of awe mixed with embarrassment and mayhap a dose of fright.

"Navy?" she guessed as her gaze followed his movements. He bent to lift his breeches from the floor before draping them over a chair and then made his way to the bed. His manhood, only partially erect, jutted out from a nest of dark curls.

"I wasn't in the military," he said as he lifted a hip onto the edge of the bed. He lay down and stretched as he inhaled deeply. A chuckle erupted as he pulled the bed linens up and over his naked body.

"What is it?" she asked as she moved to join him. She didn't remove the wrapper as she climbed onto the bed and slid beneath the covers.

"This bed is more comfortable than anything I've slept in for a very long time," he said in a quiet voice. He slipped an arm beneath her shoulders and pulled her so she was half atop him. The wrapper still hid most of her from his view, but at that moment, he was glad she wasn't naked. He needed to think. Needed her to remember.

"I don't think I've ever slept in this bed," she murmured.

He grunted. "Castlewait didn't share this bed with you?" he asked in surprise.

"He always came to mine," she replied.

"Was he good to you?"

Persephone gave a start, surprised by the query. "He wasn't a bad man. Not at all," she said in a whisper. "If he ever took a mistress, I never learned of it. He was a good father, too."

Jack jerked. "Where *are* the boys? You had... you had two, did you not?"

She hummed her initial response. "They're away at university, and my daughter is spending this Season with her grandmother in Kent," she explained, waiting for his reaction.

"You have a daughter?" he asked with a grin, wondering how he had missed learning about her.

"She'll start finishing school this autumn," Persephone said on a sigh.

"Who is seeing to the earldom?"

Persephone hesitated before saying, "I am, along with a man of business. At least until Robert is finished with university," she said, referring to her oldest son, the new Earl of Castlewait.

"You're probably doing a better job of it than he did," Jack murmured.

Furrowing a brow, Persephone sighed. "It's given me something to keep my mind occupied this past year," she admitted. "And it's really no more difficult than running the household."

Jack scoffed—he had worked in service to the Crown in order to avoid running his own earldom. Between a man of business and his solicitor and regular reports on the matter, he had to trust that the Wilmington earldom was in good stead.

"What about you?" Persephone asked. "I never heard if you married... and if you weren't in the military, what were you doing on the Continent during a war?"

Jack considered her queries and decided to answer them in order.

"Still haven't married," he replied sleepily. "Because you were the one that got away," he added before he kissed the top of her head. He grinned at hearing her soft gasp. "As for war, I worked for Chamberlain," he murmured, referring to the head of the Foreign Office. "For Crown and country and all that rot," he added.

As he expected, Persephone lifted her head from his chest to gasp, this time more forcibly. "You were a... you were *a spy?*" The last two words were barely audible. Her eyes suddenly rounded. "Do you suppose that has something to do with how you ended up in my coach this evening?"

His gaze darted to the dark fabric of the canopy above the bed. For some reason, her shock at learning he had worked for the Foreign Office had him amused. "I was." He considered her other comment. "I rather doubt my ending up in your coach has anything to do with my assignments in the Kingdom of the Netherlands, though," he murmured. He paused before he asked, "Who the hell is Lord JW?"

Still holding herself up on one elbow, Persephone ignored the curse as she stared down at Jack. She shook her head. "You mean... *you're* not?"

He rolled his eyes and winced when it caused his headache to worsen. "I am not. I mean, I am a 'Lord JW,' but I am not *the* Lord JW *The Tattler* has been writing about," he claimed.

Her gaze drifted down the counterpane as Persephone considered his words. "You're right," she murmured. "If you were on the Continent until a few weeks ago..."

"I was. When exactly did these mentions of a 'Lord JW' start appearing in print?"

Persephone didn't respond right away, her gaze on her mind's eye. "It's been a few months now, I think," she finally said.

"What was the most damning incident they wrote about?"

Persephone blinked. "Well, there was one where he allegedly climbed into a coach whilst it was stopped at an intersection and had his way with a young lady."

Jack jerked and then winced when the sudden movement had his head protesting. "He raped her?" he asked in alarm.

"No," she replied, although hesitantly. "According to the young lady's maid, the dalliance had all been arranged in advance," she explained, displaying an expression of amusement.

"Well, who was the man?"

Shrugging, she said, "The young lady wouldn't say, and neither would the lady's maid."

Jack scoffed. "What else?"

"The Kravets girl. I don't recall her given name, but she and her mother, the Baroness Kravets, were supposedly attending Lady Worthington's *musicale*, and the girl and Lord JW were discovered kissing in an alcove."

Although the incident didn't sound too damning, Jack realized kissing a young, unmarried lady could land a man in hot water. The young lady would have suffered worse, however. "When was this?" he asked.

"About a fortnight ago. I was actually in attendance that evening," Persephone said with some excitement. "It was my first time going to a Society event since burning my widow's weeds," she added with a grin.

"You burned your black gowns?" he asked in disbelief.

"To a crisp," she said, grinning in delight. "In the fireplace in my bedchamber. At least, those my lady's maid didn't want," she quickly added.

He chuckled softly, but he was more interested in what had occurred at the *musicale*. "Did you see anything? Hear anything that night?"

About to respond, she clamped her mouth shut.

"No," she finally admitted. "I don't even recall *seeing* the baroness there, which has me wondering why *The Tattler* would even make mention of her."

"They printed her *name*?" he asked in surprise.

"Well, no. Not exactly. They always just use a peer's initials, but in this case, 'Baroness K' had to be Agnes Kravets. There's no other baroness with a last name beginning with a K," she explained.

Jack furrowed a brow. "And the daughter?"

"Lady Kravets only has the one," Persephone replied.

Jack blew out a breath in frustration. "What else?"

"There have been some young widows—"

"You?" he asked, jerking as if he intended to sit up.

"I said *young* widows," Persephone repeated, pressing a hand against his chest to force him to lie down.

"You're still young," he argued.

She scoffed, but another grin touched her lips. "It's times like this I really wish you had challenged Castlewait for my hand," she whispered.

A grimace crossed his face. "As do I," he admitted.

He liked hearing her slight inhalation of breath. The way her blue eyes rounded whenever he surprised her. He closed his eyes when he felt sleep coming on, but he still had things he needed to say to her. "Over the years, I've been very good at my avocation," he said in a fading whisper. "But I've been a *terrible* aristocrat. Oh, I've attended Parliament when I can, but I don't have a wife, which means I don't have an heir, which means..." His voice trailed off as his body relaxed into the bed.

Persephone watched as he fell asleep. Although she felt the weariness of a long day, her body was well aware a naked man was pressed against her. At some point, he would awaken, and he would see to providing satiation for her swollen breasts and throbbing core.

Her racing mind was another matter, though.

If Lord JW wasn't Jack, Earl of Wilmington, then who the hell was he?

CHAPTER 7
A HAT MAKES A MAN

*E*arlier, *in front of Weatherstone Manor*

About to step up to the driver's seat of the Castlewait coach, an idea had Parker pausing. If he waited for a few minutes, he might learn the identity of the hatless man he had passed.

He placed the Earl of Wilmington's hat into the coach and made his way down the line of carriages, calling out greetings to other drivers as he took note of the gold crests on their coach doors. He recognized several as belonging to aristocrats who apparently preferred to play cards over dancing. It might be dawn before their owners took their leave of Weatherstone Manor.

"You still stargazing?" one of the older drivers chided.

"Always," he replied, giving the driver of the Marquess of Reading's coach a wave before he strolled on.

From the way the horses in front of the last coach were breathing and stomping, he knew the equipage had delivered the hatless man—none of the other beasts behaved as if they had been running in the last few mintes. He glanced up at the driver. "Haven't see you 'afore," he said. "Name's Parker."

"Thomas," the young man replied, his expression sullen. "And I'm missing me bed, as are the 'orses."

Parker gave an exaggerated shrug. "Your lordship still in the card parlor, too?" he asked, glancing back toward the house to be sure the hatless man hadn't yet emerged.

Thomas scoffed. "I wish," he replied on a huff. "Then I *would* be in me bed for the night."

"What do you mean?" Parker asked, deciding the driver had to be the one who had brought the hatless man.

"The baron didn't even attend the ball, but his business associate did. Left his hat behind," the young driver remarked with a scoff. "Thought I was going to lose me job."

"Over a hat?" Parker asked, pretending to study one of the horses.

"Over the coach not having anyone in it," Thomas replied. Younger than most drivers, he displayed cheeks pocked with acne, and his top hat looked to be entirely too large for his head.

Parker gave a start. "Who's your employer?" He glanced back towards the manor house, noting the front door had opened and a gentleman was making his exit.

"Kravets," the young driver answered, saying the name as if it were a curse. "I left *exactly* when I was supposed to," he added, holding up a chronometer. "Can't help it if some gent missed his ride to the baron's house."

Confused, Parker said, "If Lord Kravets didn't attend the ball, and your other fare missed his ride..." He paused as it dawned on him exactly what the boy meant. "Then whose hat have you come back for?"

"Mine," another voice said from behind him.

Parker whirled around to discover the hatless man from earlier approaching the coach. The short top hat Parker had returned only a few minutes before was on his head, and an expression of recognition was apparent on his face.

"You," Elias Turnbridge said as he stopped in front of Parker.

"Me, sir?" Parker replied, pretending ignorance.

"Did you... did you just return a hat to the Weatherstone house a few minutes ago?" Elias pointed to the top hat on his head. "This one?"

Parker exchanged a quick glance with Thomas. "And what if I did?"

Momentarily speechless, Elias sighed. "Well, I would wish to thank you and to ask who might have ended up with it by accident," he explained, attempting to sound reasonable. "So I could send a note of thanks," he added. "I thought it lost, you see."

Not recognizing the gentleman as someone who had seen attending Society events in the past, Parker furrowed a brow. He didn't want to tell the man he had been sent by his mistress, nor did he want to say anything about Lord Wilmington. "Well, truth be told, sir, I found it out here. On the pavement," he said, pointing in the direction from which he had come. "I like to stargaze, you see, and I nearly kicked it given the dark. I hope it's not ruined, sir."

His face falling at hearing Parker's response, Elias merely shook his head. "It's fine," he said. He sighed again. Loudly.

"What is it, sir? What's wrong?" Parker asked.

"I've lost a man," Elias stated, rolling his eyes as he realized he had no news to share with Lord Kravets. The baron would be livid when he told him he didn't know the whereabouts of Lord Wilmington.

"Sir?" Parker said, his eyes rounding in pretend shock.

*E*lias Turnbridge gave his head a shake. For a moment, he was sure he was about to learn the whereabouts of Lord Wilmington. He could barely hide his disappointment at learning his hat had been found on the pavement. "My friend was terribly drunk, you see, and in my haste to get him out of the house and into the coach, I apparently put him in the wrong coach." He glanced up at Thomas, who just then realized he was supposed to get down to open the coach door for the gentleman. "I'm surprised someone hasn't reported a stowaway," Elias added as his brows furrowed. He glanced down the line of coaches. "Unless..."

The young man jumped to the pavement next to Parker. "Sorry, sir, about all of it." He moved to open the door.

Elias held up a gloved hand to the young driver. "Start checking inside these coaches," he ordered. "My drunk friend may be in one of them." Although his expression conveyed finding the missing gentleman was still possible, Elias had already given up hope. After what the footman had said about Lord JW kissing a young lady behind a hedgerow in the gardens, he was fairly sure Lord JW and Lord Wilmington were two different people.

*P*arker exchanged a glance with the younger driver, immediately aware that Elias would not find the drunk friend in any of them. "I should get back to her ladyship's coach," Parker said as he gave the gentleman a slight bow. Although he desperately wanted to return to the Castlewait townhouse with the information he had learned, he knew he couldn't leave directly. Both the young driver and his passenger believed he was merely waiting on his mistress. "But I can help your driver look if you'd like," he offered.

"Your help would be most welcome," Elias stated.

"We can see to this, sir," Thomas said.

"All right," Elias replied. He climbed into the coach as Thomas and Parker made their way to the next coach in line.

Parker called up to Lord Reading's driver. "Any chance you have a stowaway in your coach?"

The older driver scoffed. "Not a chance. Been sitting here all night," he replied. "But you can look if you must."

Thomas opened the door and peeked in, whistling his appreciation at seeing the interior of the marquess' coach. He closed the door and they moved on to the next in line.

"This gent that was drunk... who was he?" Parker asked as they made their way.

Pausing, Thomas shrugged. "Near as I can tell, some bloke who's friends with Mr. Turnbridge."

"Turnbridge is that gentleman back there?"

Thomas nodded. "What I can't sort is how he knew the man was going to be drunk and exactly when," he remarked as they looked into the next coach. He shut the door. "I was just told to drive to the baron's house no later than half-past-ten. So I did."

Parker had no trouble pretending interest in what the young driver had to say. "Was Mr. Turnbridge in the coach at the time?"

Stopping to consider the query, Thomas frowned. "No, he wasn't."

"Well, didn't you just bring him here from the baron's house?" Parker asked, now confused.

"I did."

"Well, how did he get to the baron's house if he wasn't in the coach when you left at half-past-ten?"

Thomas waved a gloved hand. "Oh, he didn't get to the baron's house until much later," he explained. "Arrived in a hackney... mayhap an hour ago."

Parker gave a start. Turnbridge had apparently been instructed to send his drunk friend in Lord Kravets' coach and then remain at the ball. "So... when you arrived at the baron's house with the empty coach, what happened exactly?"

Thomas threw up his hands in despair. "When Lord Kravets opened the door and discovered the coach was empty, he was fit to be tied. Kept asking me where Lord Waterford...Waddleston..."

"Wilmington?" Parker offered.

"Yeah, Wilmington. He was supposed to be drunk, in the coach."

Parker grimaced. "Any idea why?" he asked before he called up to the next driver. "Can we look inside your coach? Like to see how the rich folk ride."

The driver looked up from a book he was reading by the light of a coach lantern. "Fine by me."

"Accordin' to the servants, his lordship thinks his daughter was ruint by Lord Wilmington, so he's going to make 'im marry her," Thomas said as he opened the coach door. The scent of floral perfume spilled out, which had Thomas coughing and Parker sniffing in delight.

"Well, I can tell you, it wasn't Lord Wilmington doing the ruining of Lord Kravets' daughter," Parker remarked dryly. "He's a right proper gentleman."

Thomas gave a start. "Well, if it weren't 'im, who was it?"

Parker furrowed his brows as he shut the coach door. "Well, now that's the question, isn't it?"

When the last coach—Lady Castlewait's coach—proved empty, Parker gave a shrug. "I guess Lord Kravets won't be getting a drunk Lord Wilmington on this night," he murmured.

Thomas nodded, but his attention was on the gold crest on the Castlewait coach door.

"What is it?" Parker asked, following the younger driver's line of sight.

"Looks a lot like the baron's crest is all," he said with a shrug.

Parker did his best to display a passive expression. "A little, I suppose," he replied, stunned by the similarity. Only the motto was different. "Well, you have a good night."

"Thanks for the help," Thomas replied. "I'll be getting Mr. Turnbridge home now."

"Good to meet you. I'm sure we'll see one another at future entertainments," Parker said.

He watched as the young man hurried back along the line of coaches, losing sight of him when he climbed onto the driver's seat.

As anxious as he was to drive to the Castlewait townhouse to return Lord Wilmington's top hap and tell her ladyship what he had discovered, Parker knew he would have to remain in front of the manor until long after the Kravets coach departed.

CHAPTER 8
A LADY DOES HER RESEARCH

*M*eanwhile, back at the Castlewait townhouse

Sure Jack was sound asleep, Persephone slipped from beneath the covers and crept to the mistress suite by way of the dressing room. The initials 'JW' had already brought to mind images of three aristocrats, but they were all far too old to be engaging young ladies in dark deeds in dark alcoves. Determined to learn who else might be 'Lord JW,' she pulled the counterpane from her bed, wrapped it about her shoulders, and crept out of the mistress suite and down the stairs to the library.

Turning up the flame on a candle lamp, she immediately went to the shelf containing a copy of *Debrett's Peerage and Baronetage*. Although it wasn't the most recent edition of the book of aristocrats and their families, it would do. After all, 'Lord JW' had to be of an age old enough to engage in salacious behavior, which meant he had to have been born before eighteen-hundred. More likely, he would have been born before seventeen-ninety-five.

Helping herself to a sheet of parchment, an ink pot, and a quill from her late husband's desk, she settled herself at the library table and began paging through the book. Since the initials JW could refer to a given name or to a first name and a title, she thought to start with the W's. Excitement gripped her when she discovered the first name was a candidate.

John Wainwright, Duke of Chichester.

She was about to write his name but remembered he had died in a fire. His son John had a reputation as a rake, but he, too, had died in the same fire. The younger son, Joshua, was now the duke, but he had suffered severe burns and had sequestered himself in the ducal estate in Sussex.

Persephone moved onto another page.

Wallingham, Weatherstone, Wentworth, Wessex, Whitney, Winthorpe, Wolverhampton... Not even halfway through the book, she was becoming discouraged when she noticed that the listing for the Whytes included a John.

Lord James, son of the Duke of Whyte. Too handsome for his own good, he already had a reputation as a flirt and a libertine from his days at university. From his date of birth, he would be two-and-twenty.

In the middle of writing his name on the parchment, Persephone gave a start when she heard the faint sounds of a coach pulling into the mews behind the townhouse. *That will be Parker*, she thought. She put the stopper onto the ink pot, pulled the counterpane more tightly around her shoulders, and was about to make her way to the stairs when she collided with a body larger than hers.

She nearly let out a scream until she realized it was Jack who had wrapped his arms around her.

"Apologies, my sweet," he whispered hoarsely. "I didn't mean to frighten you."

Persephone inhaled softly. "I didn't mean to wake you," she said, relieved he had found a velvet robe to wear.

"You didn't. I think your driver has returned."

"He has," she affirmed. "He's been gone long enough that he must have discovered something. Are you feeling better?" she asked, raising a hand to press it against his forehead.

"Much. I think I just had to sleep it off." He gaze darted to the library. "Whatever have you been doing?" he asked. The candle lamp was still burning, so the room was partially illuminated.

"Looking for 'Lord JW's,'" she replied as she steered them to the stairs.

"And?"

"It's only a possibility, but Lord James—"

"Whyte's whelp?" he interrupted, nearly stopping on the stairs.

"Indeed. What do you know of him?"

"Handsome, rich, and a rake. He was born the day you gifted your virtue to me."

Persephone gasped. "You remember that?"

"Twenty-two years has not dulled my memory of our week together, Sephie," he whispered hoarsely as they descended the last flight of stairs.

Touched by his words, she was about to respond when Parker appeared and stopped short at the table near the base of the stairs.

"Pardon, my lady. I... I didn't mean to wake you," he said, holding up the top hat he carried. "Your hat, my lord."

"You found it!" Jack's expression conveyed stunned surprise. "Apologies, but I don't seem to have any coins on me at the moment," he added as he patted the sides of the velvet robe.

"Oh, it was my pleasure, sir. It's been a most interesting evening."

Persephone and Jack exchanged quick glances. "Oh?" she prompted.

"We may have discovered the identity of 'Lord JW'," Jack whispered. "Do you have news?"

"Indeed," Parker said. "And I have names."

About to encourage him to continue, Persephone was prevented from doing so when Jack glanced around and lifted a finger.

"Might we move this discussion to the study?" he suggested in a quiet voice. "It appears your servant has earned a drink. Could I pour a brandy for this young man?" He turned to Parker. "You must be chilled to the bone."

The servant's eyes widened. "I... I wouldn't turn it down, sir. That is, if her ladyship doesn't mind."

"I don't mind at all." Remembering she wore only a silk robe beneath the counterpane wrapped around her shoulders, Persephone encouraged the men to precede her as they made their way to the study. Other than Bentley, no man had been in the study since Castlewait's death. She had certainly spent time in the room, though, for she had been seeing to the earldom's business for the past year.

She turned up a candle lamp but stayed in the shadows when Jack moved to the credenza behind the desk. As he saw to pouring brandy from a crystal decanter into two tumblers, he said, "Tell us what you've discovered." He lifted a glass and gave it to Parker.

"Much obliged, sir," the driver said as he took the brandy. He sniffed it, his gaze darting to Persephone. "You're sure this all right with you, my lady?" he asked as he indicated the brandy, obviously nervous.

"Only if I'm given one as well," she replied, her attention on Jack.

He chuckled as he brought her a glass. He leaned over and dropped a kiss on her head, which had Persephone gasping softly. "Jack," she scolded.

Parker pretended not to notice the earl's overt show of affection. "I spoke with one of Weatherstone's footmen. He was most apologetic about the hat, sir," Parker began. He relayed what had happened with the hatless gentleman. "While he was inside retrieving his hat, I spoke with his driver. He told me the gent's name was Turnbridge. A business associate of Lord Kravets who was sent by the baron to see to it a drunk man was put into the Kravets coach and taken to the baron's town-house no later than half-past-ten o'clock."

Persephone straightened in her chair while Jack merely furrowed his brows. "Elias Turnbridge?" he asked after a moment.

"I couldn't say for sure, sir. He never mentioned a Christian name."

Persephone scoffed. "So why did Lord Wilmington end up in *my* coach?"

Parker winced. "The coat of arms on the door of your coach is similar to that of the Kravets crest," he replied. "And Mr. Turnbridge didn't actually put his lordship into the coach. Apparently the two commoners I noticed hanging about the bushes were lackeys of the baron. They were the ones who put you into her lady-ship's coach," he explained as he turned to Jack.

The earl's attention was on Persephone, though. "You mentioned Kravets had a daughter who was caught kissing in an alcove at Worthington House," he prompted.

"Honoria," she said, remembering the young lady's name. "According to *The Tattler*," she added. She took a sip of the brandy and closed her eyes as the warm liquid slid down her throat. "I suppose Kravets expected to kidnap you as a means to force a marriage to her."

"Well, that wasn't going to happen," Jack groused. He turned his attention back on Parker. "Did Kravets' driver suspect anything?"

"No, sir. I pretended her ladyship was still inside the Weatherstone house, and I even waited until they were well on their way before I returned here. To keep up the ruse."

"Good thinking. What about Turnbridge?"

Parker shrugged. "He seemed most concerned about what Baron Kravets would do to him. He fears him, I think. Said the baron would be livid if he returned without you."

"Who *is* this Turnbridge?" Persephone asked, sure she hadn't heard the name mentioned before.

"He's an inventor," Jack stated. "Always looking for someone to back his latest venture." He cursed under his breath. "He was with me at the punchbowl. Speaking to me about some sort of steam-powered invention. He was looking for investors. I pretended interest if only because I've been away from England so long, I wished to learn what I'd missed," he added with a shake of his head.

"He must have put a sleeping powder in your punch, sir," Parker said. "Which is why he has to be wondering how 'Lord JW' was able to ravish another young lady behind a hedgerow in the Weatherstone gardens later in the evening."

Jack and Persephone stared at the driver. "What's this?" Jack asked.

"When I was making conversation with the footman, he mentioned there had been an incident right before the midnight supper was announced. 'Lord JW' was caught kissing a young lady behind a hedgerow," he repeated. "Said he was a rake and that he'd been caught with a number of young ladies since his return from his Grand Tour, which means that 'Lord JW' has to be younger than you, sir." He paused a moment. "No offense, sir."

Throwing his head back, Jack guffawed. "I've a mind to take Lord James with me when I pay a call on Lord Kravets tomorrow," he said before he drained his brandy. "Maybe the duke, too."

"You're going to confront Kravets?" Persephone asked, stunned by his words.

"I am," he affirmed. "Might Mr. Parker be allowed to drive me in the afternoon? I rather imagine I'm going to be abed well past twelve," he said as his eyes darted to the clock on the fireplace mantel.

"I'm going with you," Persephone announced.

Jack blinked before he regarded her with an assessing glance. "If you're sure," he said.

"Oh, I'm sure," she replied. "Mr. Parker, I shall see to it there's something extra in your pay this month for all your trouble."

"Why, thank you, my lady. I didn't mind doing it at all."

"Well, don't be getting any ideas about becoming a

Bow Street Runner," Jack remarked. "This household can already boast a former spy."

Parker's eyes rounded. "Sir?"

Persephone inhaled softly, but she didn't say anything as Jack raised his empty glass to the driver. "I am retired, and I am ready to resume my duties as an earl," he said before setting the glass on the salver behind the desk. "After I get a good night's sleep."

"Yes, sir," Parker said, doing the same with his glass. "My lady," he said. He bowed and took his leave of the study.

Persephone made no move to rise from her chair, deciding she should wait until Parker had made it down the corridor and up the servants' stairs to his quarters. "A good night's sleep?" she repeated softly.

Jack moved to stand before her and then bent to lift her from the chair. "Eventually," he whispered. He kissed her forehead and then wrapped his ams around her shoulders. "After I've done to you what I've been accused of doing to others these past few weeks."

Persephone glanced up at him, the heat at her core due to more than just the brandy. "I look forward to it," she whispered.

After several minutes of kissing, the two returned to the master suite.

CHAPTER 9
A TRUTH IS UNWELCOME

Meanwhile, at the Kravets townhouse

Dreading his next conversation with Baron Kravets, Elias stepped down from the coach and gave Thomas a beseeching look. "I hate to keep you, but I should only be a moment," he called up to the driver.

Thomas tipped his hat. "I'll wait, sir."

Elias didn't expect a butler to open the door for him, so he was surprised when it did—he hadn't even crossed over the area when Lord Kravets appeared in the opening. "I see you found your hat," the barrel-chested baron groused.

"It was mistakenly given to another and had been returned only moments before I got there," Elias replied, gingerly stepping into the vestibule.

"And Wilmington?"

"He is not 'Lord JW'."

Kravets, garbed in a thick, dark banyan, drew his head back and scoffed. "He tell you that?"

Elias shook his head. "'Lord JW' was found kissing a young lady behind a hedgerow. Before the midnight supper was served," he said as they made their way into the study.

"That's impossible," Kravets replied. "If he drank even half of the sleeping powder you put in his glass of punch, there's no way he could have awakened before midnight," he claimed.

"Exactly," Elias stated. "I watched him. He drank all of it." He waited a moment to allow Kravets to do his own reasoning before he said, "'Lord JW' is not Wilmington, sir. In fact, he's a young man. Described as being in his early twenties, at least according to the footman who relayed the information."

"That's... that cannot be," Kravets said, shaking his head.

"Why not? 'Lord JW' only ravishes young ladies and young widows."

Still not convinced, Kravets poured a glass of brandy and nearly downed it in one gulp. Still chilled from his late night foray to Weatherstone Manor, Elias was glad when the baron poured a glass for him, too. "Much obliged, sir." He savored the smoky aroma before he took a drink. His gaze settled on the amber liquid for a moment. "I had your driver check the other coaches that were still parked in front of Weatherstone Manor, just to be sure Lord Wilmington wasn't in any of them."

"Which means he went home with someone," Kravets groused. His eyes suddenly widened. "Will he remember *you* were the one who helped him out of the ballroom?" he asked.

Elias had been fearing the very same. Would the Earl of Wilmington remember their brief conversation as Elias handed him a glass of punch? He had seemed interested in learning more about his latest application for a steam engine—a sort of dog cart that would allow its user to push heavy crates around without the need for horses or muscle-bound laborers.

"He might," Elias hedged, "but if he should see me again, I'll do my best to avoid him, and if I cannot…" He allowed the sentence to trail off. "I'll say I noticed he didn't seem to be feeling well."

"Probably for the best," Kravets murmured. "Well, I don't know about you, but I'm going to bed."

Relieved to hear he was being dismissed, Elias set his empty glass on the edge of the desk. "Thank you for the brandy. I look forward to receiving your bank draft for the investment," he said, before giving the baron a bow. He took his leave of the townhouse.

Thomas had stepped down from the driver's bench and stood next to the coach door, his attention on the crest.

"What's wrong?" Elias asked, pausing to follow the driver's gaze.

"Oy, nothing, sir. I was just thinking about how

similar this crest is to the one on the coach of that driver we was talking to earlier."

Weary from the long night, Elias merely shrugged and climbed into the coach. Nearly lulled to sleep by the sound of the wheels and the hooves of the horses on the cobblestones, Elias gave a start when the coach stuttered to a stop in front of The Albany.

Elias was about to step out of the coach when the significance of the driver's words hit him. He glanced at the Kravets crest before giving a nod to Thomas.

About to ask as to the identity of the other driver, Elias decided he didn't want to know.

CHAPTER 10
AN EARL CLAIMS HIS FUTURE COUNTESS

*M*eanwhile, back at the Castlewait townhouse

Anticipation. Excitement. Trepidation. Nervousness.

All of these and more had Persephone trembling when she and Jack were finally back in the master suite. She slid a hand along the collar of his velvet robe to push it from his shoulder, her palm barely touching his heated skin.

He inhaled sharply at her caress and lifted the hand from where it smoothed over the bare skin above his upper chest. "I apologize for having fallen asleep earlier. We were discussing important matters."

"It's all right," she whispered, using her free hand to push the robe from his other shoulder. She had expected they would already be on the bed. Wished he was atop her and doing to her what he had so masterfully done all those years ago. The pleasure he had imparted had been extraordinary. Intense and all-consuming. Intoxicating. "I'm rather surprised you could sound so coherent after what you suffered this evening."

He kissed her lips and then her jaw. "I had more to say," he whispered. "I *have* more to say."

When one of his hands smoothed over a silk-covered breast to gently mold it, Persephone nearly jerked from his hold. "Could we maybe talk afterwards?"

Jack chuckled as he pulled back to regard her with an expression of curiosity. "You're trembling," he said, sobering.

"Of course I am. You have me..." Her hand slid down the front of his body until it reached the nest of curls above his turgid manhood. Her fingers slid around the base of his member and gently squeezed. The skin there felt as velvety as the robe that had fallen to his feet.

One of his hands briefly covered hers as he groaned his appreciation. "Aroused?" he guessed. His hand let go of hers, the palm sliding between her thighs to discover the dark curls were already damp. He used his middle finger to press against her swollen womanhood, jerking when she tightened her hold on him at the same moment she cried out.

If he didn't get her on the bed right now, they would end up on the floor.

"Come, my sweet," he whispered, pulling her hand from his member so he could lift her into his arms. He placed her on the bed and undid the bow that held her silk wrapper closed. Peeling the edges apart, he lowered his head to one breast and kissed its engorged nipple.

"I already have. Now it's *your* turn," she said, her hand once again reaching for his manhood.

He chuckled at her comment, finally climbing onto the bed so he hovered over her. "You do know that there will be repercussions?" he murmured, before his mouth covered the other breast.

Persephone jerked as she moved her hands to the sides of his head, her thumbs at his temples. "Repercussions?" she repeated, giving a start when his teeth gently bit her nipple.

"Yes, my Sephie. You're going to marry me," he said, moving his kisses down the front of her body and one hand to the space between her thighs.

She inhaled sharply. "Why do make it sound so...? Oh!"

Jack chuckled into her belly, which had her squirming. "You're going to be my countess," he said. He had her knees spread wide and his mouth pressed against one thigh.

"You make it... sound so... so *ominous*," she responded between gasps for air. When his tongue touched her womanhood and circled it, she hummed as her head arched back into the pillow. Sure he was going to leave her on the precipice of a release she desperately needed unless she gave him an answer, she mewled and said, "It would be my honor."

He shoved his tongue inside her, the rough texture

sending her over the edge of the precipice and into an ocean of pleasure waves. Although she didn't know where one began and another ended, Jack certainly seemed to. He was up and over her, burying his cock into her at the very moment another wave of pleasure crashed.

Persephone's knees gripped his thighs as he thrust into her over and over. When his body suddenly stilled and the cords of his neck appeared in relief as he lifted his head, she knew he had finally allowed his own release. Heat filled her lower body.

Knowing what to do to prolong his pleasure, she tightened her inner muscles so she gripped him harder. She slid a hand down the side of his body until her fingertips could reach his stiff sac to lift it. She hummed when he jerked in her hold and grinned when she heard his quiet curse before he finally, slowly, lowered himself to lay half atop her.

His head landed on the pillow between her neck and shoulder. "Damn, but I've missed you," he whispered. A moment later, and his body relaxed.

At first, Persephone was sure he had fallen asleep, so she was surprised when his lips captured her earlobe and gently nibbled it. She gave a start and then purred. "I've missed you as well."

They lay quietly for a few minutes, Persephone well aware when his manhood finally softened. Jack lifted himself from her body and rolled onto the bed, one arm bent and landing above his head while he slid the other behind her shoulders to pull her against his side. She expected he had fallen asleep, so she was startled when he turned and kissed the top of her head.

"I didn't mean for my proposal to sound so... so daunting," he murmured.

She grinned. "I was curious about that," she admitted.

He tightened his hold on her. "You've been running the Castlewait earldom until your son is old enough?"

Surprised by the change in topic, she shrugged in his hold. "I have. It's no different from running the household," she replied on a sigh. "Arrange goods and services where needed. Pay the invoices. Keep a ledger."

Chuckling softly, Jack asked, "Will you help me with mine?"

She angled her head in the small of his shoulder so she could better see him. "Of course."

He kissed her on the lips and then settled his head back into the pillow.

Once again, Persephone was sure he had gone to sleep when he said, "Am I mad to think I should give Kravets some sort of gift when I pay a call on him later today?"

Persephone lifted herself onto an elbow and stared down at him. "Whatever for?" she asked in alarm.

Jack shrugged in the pillow. "Well, if it wasn't for him, we wouldn't be here. Like this," he said.

Scoffing, she stared at him as if he were mad. "If it wasn't for him, we would have found one another during the ball tonight," she countered. "We would have danced

—twice—and we would have ended up in the gardens, where I would have invited you to join me in my bed before the supper was served." She huffed. "We could have made love two or three times by now."

Jack regarded her for a long moment, a grin spreading over his face as he pondered her words. "All right. So no gift for the baron," he said. He lifted himself onto an elbow and kissed her. "Maybe I'll plant a facer on him instead."

A snort erupted from Persephone. "If you don't, I will."

He let out a guffaw. "I'm so glad I ended up in your coach. And I promise I'll make up for the lost time later," he murmured.

Giving him a prim grin, Persephone lowered herself back onto the bed. "I don't know about you, but I'm looking forward to life with you."

He chuckled again as he collapsed back onto the bed and wrapped his arms around her. "I'll remember you said that when you learn the state of my earldom," he murmured.

A few seconds later, and he was sound asleep.

Persephone would have joined him in slumber, but his last remark had her worried. Concerned. Nervous and excited.

Challenge accepted, she thought as she dozed off.

CHAPTER 11
AN EARL AND HIS LADY PAY
A CALL

*E**arly afternoon*

Jack held a hand for Persephone as she stepped up and into the Castlewait coach. Despite the gloves they both wore, he felt a welcome warmth when their hands touched.

Parker closed the door behind him once he was seated next to her.

"What is it?" Persephone asked as she settled into the velvet squabs. Despite having spent only the past night with one another after so many years apart, she knew something was bothering the earl.

"Nothing. Everything." He sighed as he straightened in the squabs. "Thank you for insisting on coming with me," he added before he reached an arm behind her shoulders.

Since the hat she wore was pinned at a jaunty angle, she was able to rest her head on his shoulder. "I take it the light of day has you reconsidering what you were thinking to do in the middle of the night?"

Jack frowned. "What? If you mean that I'm not as inclined to throttle Kravets—"

"Not that," she interrupted with a bemused expression.

His mind cycled through everything he had said whilst they had discovered the most likely 'Lord JW' candidate. What they had talked about with Parker. What they had talked about in bed.

"Are you having second thoughts about marrying me?" Jack asked in alarm.

Persephone lifted her head from his shoulder and regarded him with surprise. "Aren't you?"

His eyes rounded. "No. I thought... well, that is, if you hadn't changed your mind, I thought that perhaps we might secure a marriage license after I'm finished with the baron."

Leaning away from Jack until her shoulder hit the coach wall, she tittered. "I haven't changed my mind," she said.

He grinned. "Good."

"Have you decided what you're going to say to the baron?"

Jack allowed a shrug. "Well, I thought I would start with admonishing him. Threaten him with bodily harm. And then, after he groveled enough, I would begrudgingly forgive him since his arrangements meant we were reunited, but in a less than optimal manner that would have happened if he hadn't been involved in his nefarious scheme in the first place." He paused as he regarded her with a questioning glance. "Does that sound reasonable?"

Persephone had a gloved hand covering her mouth as she laughed. "Poor Lord Kravets," she murmured. "His wife, Margaret, is never going to forgive him if *The Tattler* learns what he's done."

"Oh...," Jack breathed. "Is that possible?" he asked, his brows furrowed.

"I could mention the circumstances over afternoon tea in someone's parlor," she hinted. "One never knows who's a contributor to that rag."

He gave her a grin. "Remind me never to anger you."

"I will if I must," she teased.

After a few minutes of contemplation, Jack inhaled softly. "I'm still curious as to why Mr. Turnbridge was involved," he said absently.

"Well, you mentioned he was an inventor in need of investors," she reminded him. "Perhaps the baron saw an opportunity to make the poor man work for his money."

"Could be," Jack agreed. "Which means it's rather doubtful Turnbridge would ever speak to me again."

"He wouldn't dare, unless it's to apologize," she agreed.

The coach stuttered to a halt, and they both straightened in the squabs. When Parker opened the door, they stepped down and walked arm in arm to the front door of the Kravets townhouse.

When the butler opened the blue door, he gave a nod and stepped back.

Jack pulled a calling card from his waistcoat pocket. "Lord—"

"Lady Castlewait," Persephone interrupted, her gloved hand held out. A white pasteboard calling card was clutched between her thumb and forefinger. "Could you let Lord Kravets know I wish to speak with him, please?"

His gaze darting between Jack and Persephone, the butler took another step back. "I'll see if he's in residence, my lady."

When the servant had disappeared through a door further into the hall, Jack whispered, "What are you doing?"

"Securing us an audience with the baron," she replied. "Although you are a very handsome man, I think Lord Kravets is more inclined to agree to see me than you."

Jack's head fell back on his neck as he guffawed. "God, she's clever, too," he whispered.

When Abraham Kravets emerged from his study, his pleasant expression faltered when he realized Persephone wasn't alone. "Lady Castlewait," he said by way of greeting, taking her gloved hand to his lips. When he straightened, he furrowed a brow when his attention went to Jack. "Lord Wilmington. Haven't seen you much of late," he said, his nervousness apparent.

"That's because I've been on the Continent, Kravets.

Working for King and country and all that rot," he replied, his manner testy. "I've only been back in London for a fortnight." He arched a brow to emphasize the last word.

Kravets rocked back on his heels as his expression held a hint of fear. "A... a fortnight, you say?"

"Aye. It seems in my absence, Lord Whyte's whelp, James, has been doing dirty deeds in dark places and getting caught by whoever provides the *on-dit* to that damned *Tattler* rag," Jack stated. He turned his head in Persephone's direction and said, "Pardon the curse, my sweet."

"Oh, you're pardoned," she said brightly, her gaze darting beyond the baron to see that his baroness, Patience, had come down the stairs. She was no doubt curious as to the identity of her husband's callers.

Jack continued his scold. "And you had the audacity to think that your daughter would have anything to do with a man old enough to be her father during a *musicale* at Lady Worthington's house?"

Kravets' mouth opened and shut a few times, making him appear much like a fish.

"You do realize that marrying your daughter off to a duke's son would be a far superior choice than to an earl who is old enough to be her father?" Jack went on, well aware Lady Kravets was in the hall beyond her husband, wringing her hands in front of her chest as if she feared for his life.

"Well, I hadn't because.... because everyone said *you* were 'Lord JW'," Kravets finally blurted.

"Well, I am not," Jack countered, allowing his anger to show. "Do you know how upsetting this has been for my betrothed?"

"Betrothed?" the baron repeated, blinking.

"That would be me," Persephone said in a hoarse whisper. "Imagine my *shock* when my intended was drugged and forcibly removed from the Weatherstone ballroom last night. Why, if your henchmen hadn't mistaken my coach for yours, I would have had to hire a Bow Street Runner to find my 'Lord JW,' and then, when the banns were read for your daughter's wedding, I would have had to put voice to my objection," she claimed, her annoyance apparent. "Imagine the gossip. Imagine the scandal. There isn't a man in this town who would dare ask Honoria for her hand after that."

While Patience let out a quiet cry of fright, Kravets audibly gulped. "I... I didn't know," he said with a shake of his head. "I swear. What must I do to make this right?"

Not expecting an offer of contrition, Persephone glanced up at Jack. He was apparently as surprised as she was.

"You... you can pay for our marriage license," Jack suggested.

Kravets looked momentarily stunned. "I'll see to it. A special license, if you'd like," he said, his eyes still round.

"You won't tell anyone, will you?" Patience asked, rushing forward to stand next to her husband. "I had no idea what he did," she claimed, punching Kravets in the arm to punctuate her claim. "But my daughter shouldn't have to suffer for his wrongs."

Persephone reached out a gloved hand to take one of the baroness'. "Oh, Lady Kravets, I assure you, Honoria's honor will not suffer further from us," she said. "But I do think Lord Wilmington has the right idea with his suggestion that your daughter be betrothed to Lord James as soon as possible. That is, if you don't mind having a rake for a son-in-law."

Lady Kravets' face screwed up in a grimace before she sighed. "Well, he is a duke's son," she countered, as if his aristocratic relationship was enough to overcome the young man's reputation. "And the heir."

"Well, there is that. And he is rather handsome," Persephone added. She ignored Jack's jerk at hearing the comment, but turned to glance up at him, giving him a wink that she hoped would calm him.

When his brows furrowed, she asked, "What is it?"

"Was Honoria at the Weatherstone ball last night?" Jack asked of the baron.

"Why, yes," Kravets replied after a pause, his gaze darting to his wife. Patience gave a quick nod of acknowledgement.

"Was she with Lord James behind a hedgerow in the gardens before the midnight supper was served?"

The baroness gasped as her eyes rounded. The baron seemed to pale. "Why... what do you know?"

Jack inhaled to answer, but it was Persephone who

said, "Since the Weatherstone footmen knew of it, the editor of *The Tattler* is sure to know of it. The next issue comes out tomorrow, so I would suggest that if it was Honoria behind the hedgerow with Lord James—"

"I know what to do," Kravets stated. He lifted his chin. "Let the archbishop's office know I'll pay for your license at the same time I'll be seeing to one for my daughter and Lord James," he stated. "Patience," he turned to his wife, "Have our daughter dressed and down here in a half-hour."

The baroness curtsied and hurried up the stairs.

Persephone and Jack exchanged quick glances. "Very well," Jack murmured. "I'll see you in the next session of Parliament." He nodded as Persephone curtsied, and the two turned to take their leave. Before they were over the threshold, though, Jack paused and said, "Oh, and do be sure to fund Mr. Turnbridge's latest venture."

Kravets frowned. "I don't know what you mean," he responded.

Scowling, Jack said, "Oh, I think you do. Good day." He tipped his hat as he offered his arm to Persephone.

CHAPTER 12
NEWLYWEDS READ THE GOSSIP

The following week in the master suite of the Castlewait townhouse

As Persephone lounged in the pillows and drank her cup of chocolate, her new husband was paging through the latest issue of *The Tattler*.

"Do people really believe this rot?" Jack asked, scoffing.

His new wife arched a brow. "I would not expect you of all people to ask that," she countered with a grin.

He captured one of her hands in his and raised it to his lips. Kissing the back of it, he squeezed it tighter. "I suppose it merely depends on who you imagine these initials to be," he murmured, already engrossed in another article about the Weatherstone ball.

"Have you found a mention of our marriage in there?" she asked, leaning against his shoulder in an effort to read an advertisement for a New Bond Street modiste.

He gave a start. "They write about weddings in here?"

She tittered. "Of course, darling. Why wouldn't they?"

"I wouldn't expect them to be scandalous enough," he mused.

"Well, ours might appear that way given how quick it was," she countered.

He chuckled. "Who knew you could obtain a special license and be married all in the same day?" he asked rhetorically.

Persephone smirked but didn't respond.

"I do hope you don't regret it," Jack murmured, his gaze lifting from the news-sheet to regard her with worry.

"So far, I'm a very happy bride," she said before kissing him on the cheek. "But then I haven't seen the ledgers for your earldom yet."

He winced. "Let's wait until after our wedding trip before I subject you to the Wilmington earldom," he murmured.

"Oooh. A wedding trip?"

"Hmm. I was thinking of taking you to my country estate," he said, his attention still on the news-sheet.

"Oooh, in what country?" she teased.

He chuckled. "If I tell you that, it won't be a surprise," he said. He suddenly straightened, aiming the news-sheet so she could better see it. "Well, well," he whispered.

"What is it?" She followed his gaze to an article and grinned.

It is with much excitement that we announce the betrothal of Lord James, son of the Duke of Whyte, to Miss Honoria Kravets, daughter of the Baron and Lady Kravets. We've reported on this couple's exploits in past issues—they've been caught fondling one another at a number of Society entertainments—so it comes as no surprise that this Lord JW would finally be brought to task. He was said to be honored to offer for Honoria's hand and hopes for a quick wedding so that they might canoodle whenever they wish.

"Patience will be mortified to read this," Persephone murmured. "Honoria is her only daughter." She waited for Jack to reply, but he was still reading, his grin widening.

Curious, she continued where she had left off.

As for another, older Lord JW—who hasn't been seen in London for some time (rusticating in the country, perhaps? Or mayhap he's been serving King and country on the Continent?)—it seems a wedding is in his very near future. A special license was issued only yesterday, but we've yet to discover who he plans to wed. About time this earl be married. He's not getting any younger.

"You might not be getting any younger, but your new wife certainly doesn't mind," Persephone whispered as she slipped a hand beneath the bed linens. She covered his manhood with her palm, not surprised when it twitched and hardened beneath her hold.

"I rather like that you seem to enjoy canoodling," Jack remarked, setting aside the news-sheet. "Imagine the scandal when we're caught in a dark alcove canoodling during a *musicale*."

"Or making love in the gardens during a ball," she whispered.

"Or in our box at the theatre," he countered.

"We have a box?" she asked in surprise.

He chuckled as he gripped the edge of the bed linens and flipped them off the both of them. Persephone giggled when he lifted his body over hers. "We have a box," he affirmed. "But first..." He thrust himself into her and sighed with pleasure. "I'm going to abduct you..." He pulled out and kissed her throughly before thrusting into her again, groaning when her hips met his. "And take you to my house in the country..." He pulled out, but not all the way. "Where I intend to get a child on you..."

Persephone moved her hands to his buttocks, and she pulled on him hard enough so he was caught by surprise as her hips lifted to meet his. "If you haven't already," she finished for him, her face glowing in the morning light.

She adored how he kissed her then, the same way he had done so all those years ago when they had first fallen in love. When he finally ended the kiss, he stared down at her.

"What is it?" she asked in a whisper.

"Is that even possible?" he asked, breathless.

She blinked. "Well, of course." When he didn't resume what he'd been doing before their kiss, she added, "But please, do continue. Just to be sure."

His face split into a grin, and he kissed her again. "Gladly."

EPILOGUE

Two years later, at the Wilmington country estate, Cheshire

His attention on the ledger spread open on his oak desk, Jack entered numbers matching those on an invoice he held in his other hand. Although he hadn't excelled at simple arithmetic as a student at Eton, he had discovered he was far better at keeping the books for his earldom than he had expected.

He was also coming to the realization that he was interested in farming, at least to the point of learning about planting, crop rotation, farm implements, and irrigation techniques. Since he owned several books on the topic, he had read them all. As for actually doing the farming, he thought it best to leave that to his tenants. Since he was sure he couldn't keep a house plant alive, he doubted he could mange a field of wheat.

Having met all his tenant farmers in person, he had

also discovered he rather liked knowing a bit about their lives. Accompanied by his countess, he met their wives and children as they delivered baskets of food and gifts for Christmas. He was invited to their weddings and was sure to be present for their baby's christenings.

The wedding trip he and Persephone had taken to the Wilmington country estate was still ongoing. If it had been up to him, it might never end, but he was prepared to do his duty as an earl and attend Parliament. Squire his countess about the capital to attend the usual Society entertainments.

When the new Earl of Castlewait finished university and took his seat in Parliament, Jack and Persephone would move out of the Castlewait townhouse and into another one Persephone had found only one street away.

Shortly after he had finally taken his bride, Jack had met with his earldom's man of business, J. Arthur Peabody. Expecting the worst, he had learned that all was well. There was income from his farmland, expenses were reasonable, and maintenance had been done on buildings when it was required.

"There is one way you might increase your income," the man of business had remarked upon their last meeting.

"Oh?" Jack had responded.

"There is an inventor, one Elias Turnbridge, who has come up with a rather unique application for a steam engine," Mr. Peabody said. "For a small investment of one-hundred pounds, you could see your money doubled in only a year's time."

Persephone, who had been sitting next to him during the meeting, hid her mouth with a gloved hand but said nothing as Jack merely stared at Mr. Peabody.

"Sir?" his man of business had prompted.

Jack cleared his throat. "I am not interested," he stated.

Apparently surprised by the response, Mr. Peabody had merely shrugged and moved on to other business.

It was after that meeting that Jack decided to see to the business of the earldom himself.

The sound of babbling had him glancing up from the invoice to discover his countess standing on the threshold of his study. Dressed in an aquamarine day gown of muslin, she looked as gorgeous as the day they had married. A moment later, and he was thinking of how she had looked that morning, her sleep tousled hair hiding one eye as she kissed him awake.

He always enjoyed what happened a few minutes later, when he slowly made love to her, or when she climbed atop him and rode him to a quick and satisfying release. Mornings as a married man were far better than his days as a bachelor.

"Well, good morning, my sweet. Is it already time for tea?" he asked.

She grinned and seemed to stutter-step into the

study. "Probably, but there's something far more important for you to see."

"Oh?" He stood from the desk and realized almost immediately what she meant.

His son and heir, John Junior, dressed in a long gown, was standing rather unsteadily in front of his mother. Chubby fingers were wrapped around Persephone's forefingers as the babe took a tentative step forward. A grin split his face at the sight of his father, and more babbling ensued as he took another unsteady step.

"Is that my son?" Jack asked in surprise.

"Well, I should hope so," Persephone replied with a scoff. "He's most certainly mine."

"Well, every time I see him, he's taller," Jack said in his own defense. "And now he has teeth." He returned to his seat so his outstretched arms were more level with the year-old boy. "But he's not bald anymore."

Persephone tittered. "You see him every day," she scolded as the babe let go of his hold on her fingers and lurched forward. Three steps later, and he was in his father's arms, babbling incoherently. Tears of joy pricked the corners of her eyes. "Oh, my darlings," she whispered.

Jack lifted the boy into the air and stood. John giggled and spread his arms wide as his father swooped him through the air. "What shall I teach you first, young man?" Jack asked as he settled back into his chair. "Your mother tells me you're already a consummate flirt."

Enjoying the show her husband was putting on for her, Persephone crossed her arms and leaned against the door frame. "You might warn him about fast girls," she suggested. "Remind him to be wary lest he be abducted and forced into a marriage."

Jack glanced at her in alarm. "You make it sound as if that's what happened to me," he countered.

Her eyes darting sideways, Persephone decided it best she not to remind him that in a somewhat roundabout manner, that's exactly what had happened to him.

ABOUT THE AUTHOR

A self-described nerd and student of history, Linda Rae spent many years as a published technical writer specializing in 3D graphics workstations, software and 3D animation (her movie credits include *SHREK* and *SHREK 2*). Getting lost in the rabbit holes of research has resulted in historical romances set in the Regency-era as well as Ancient Greece.

A fan of action-adventure movies, she can frequently be found at the local cinema. Although she no longer has any tropical fish, she follows the San Jose Sharks and makes her home in Cody, Wyoming.

For more information:
www.lindaraesande.com
Sign up for Linda Rae's newsletter:
Regency Romance with a Twist
Follow Linda Rae's blog:
Regency Romance with a Twist